The Susie K Diaries

Happy Camper!

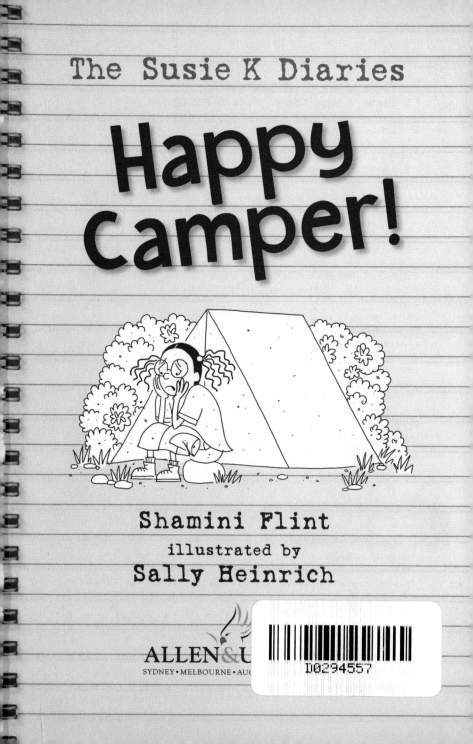

Shamini Flint

illustrated by
Sally Heinrich

ALLEN&U
SYDNEY • MELBOURNE • AUC

For Frans, always my happy camper. SF
For Sophie, a happy camper whatever she does! X SH

First published by Allen & Unwin in 2019

Allen & Unwin
83 Alexander Street
Crows Nest NSW 2065
Australia
Phone: (61 2) 8425 0100
Email: info@allenandunwin.com
Web: www.allenandunwin.com

A catalogue record for this
book is available from the
National Library of Australia

ISBN 978 1 76052 828 7

For teaching resources, explore
www.allenandunwin.com/resources/for-teachers

Cover design by Sandra Nobes
Text design by Sally Heinrich
Set in Gel Pen Upright Light by Sandra Nobes
This book was printed in November 2018 by McPherson's Printing Group, Australia.

10 9 8 7 6 5 4 3 2 1

Name:
THE SUSIE K DIARIES
HAPPY CAMPER!

File No. #4

CONFIDENTIAL

Case Opened

My name is Susie K.
I like to be by myself in a quiet corner reading
a book with my skeleton, Bones, and my
best friend, George,
the school goldfish.

But Mum wants me to be a huge success at
everything I do.

Well, this time Mum has gone too far...

Imagine you're afraid of dogs...and you find yourself surrounded by every sort of BIG DOG in the world.

AND you still have to finish your homework...

Well, it's worse than that...

Imagine you're afraid of heights and you find yourself on a tall ladder on a tall tree on a tall mountain.

And there's a leopard on the ladder with you...

Well, it's worse than that!!!

Imagine, you're afraid of water…and you find yourself in a small boat in the middle of a ginormous ocean.

And the ocean is on another planet…

Well, it's worse than that!!!!

6

9

I don't want to be a happy camper.
I like it at home...

I like to sleep in my bed,

in my bedroom,

in my house,

with Bones,

and George...

IS THAT TOO MUCH TO ASK????

Let's find out...

Mum, I'm not sure camping is my thing...

Of course it is! You'll learn so much that might be useful to you in real life!!!

Like what???

I remember when I was a child, if I had known how to light a fire in the wild, we could have stayed warm when we were escaping from the soldiers!!!

Every single time, EVERY SINGLE TIME...
when I don't want to do something Mum tells me
what it was like when she was a child refugee!!
How is anyone supposed to argue with that? SIGH...

Mum and I have something in common. We both like
to know stuff.

Did you know that the
bend in a flamingo's leg
isn't a knee –
it's an ankle??

Did you know that goats
have rectangular pupils?

Did you know that a
group of pugs
is called a grumble?

But Mum also wants me to know STUFF that will be USEFUL IN EMERGENCIES!!!

If she had her wish, I would know so much STUFF I would know how to survive...

the zombie apocalypse...

the attack of the vampires...

the return of the dinosaurs...

But I don't even know how to...

boil an egg...

tie my hair neatly...

find my way out of a
paper bag...

And now I have to SURVIVE in the WILD!!!

Nope, not going to happen.

It's survival of the fittest, Susie K, not the nerdiest.

George and Jack are right.

There is ZERO chance I will survive in the WILD.

I need to find a way of fixing this problem...

And that, my friends, is exactly what I am going to do!

BECAUSE I am a PROBLEM SOLVER!!!!

Even better, I already have a system that works.

1) identify the problem
2) analyse the problem
3) find d solution
4) test the solution
5) repeat until THE PROBLEM IS SOLVED.

The method to solve all problems, whatever they might be, is exactly the same...

1. IDENTIFY THE PROBLEM

That's easy...Mum wants me to be a HAPPY CAMPER!!!

And I only know how to be the world's saddest, unhappiest, most miserable CAMPER...

Why don't they have a camp for that?

2. ANALYSE THE PROBLEM

It is not possible for me to actually survive in the wild.

I do not run fast, so I will not be able to get away from predators...

I do not climb trees, so I will not be able to get away from predators...

And my eyesight is bad, so if I lose my glasses
I won't be able to spot predators...

3. FIND A SOLUTION

The next day at school...

Or do I?

Maybe I should run away from home?

Just George and me and Bones...

What are you doing, Susie K?
Running away from home...
To get out of this camping trip?
What else?
Where are you going?
Far, far away...
Over hill and mountains...
Across rivers and waterfalls...
until we're safe in the middle of a deep dark wood where no one can find us...
You're going to run away from a camping trip in the jungle...
by going camping in the jungle?
Bwahahahahahahahaha!!

Mr Robinson, the camp instructor, said the first test of our survival skills would be packing for the trip.

Bring everything to school tomorrow and I'll check that you're prepared for this trip.

What do I need to pack?

I've got it!!

If you can't avoid the wild, maybe the solution is to take a little piece of home with you...

George
Bones
Bug catcher
Sudoku book
Dictionary
Encyclopedia
Chemistry set
— test tubes
— chemicals
— bunsen burner
Computer
Printer
Scanner
Magnifying glass
Microscope
Telescope
Umbrella
Crossword book

4. TEST THE SOLUTION

The next day at school...

27

I'm in terrible trouble. Clementine is too.

We have to squeeze everything we need into a single rucksack.

DAY 1 OF CAMP

The day dawned bright and early.

The sun was shining...

The birds were singing...

The parents were excited...

The kids were packed...

We got on the bus...

We drove for miles...

And then we were dropped off at the edge of the forest...

What is Bill doing?
Now you see me,
now you don't.
See me!
Don't see me!!
See!!!
Don't!!!!
What in the world is the matter with you?
I'm practising...
my survival skills...

That evening, I decided that camping was easy.

I helped set up the tents...

I toasted marshmallows...

We sang songs around the campfire...

DAY 2 OF CAMP

45

Where are you going, Clementine?
Where do you think I'm going?
Oh.
Well, you shouldn't go on your own. You might get lost.
I'm not an idiot.
You can't handle the truth!
Why are you bringing the fish?
Fish are friends, not food. I don't trust Bill...

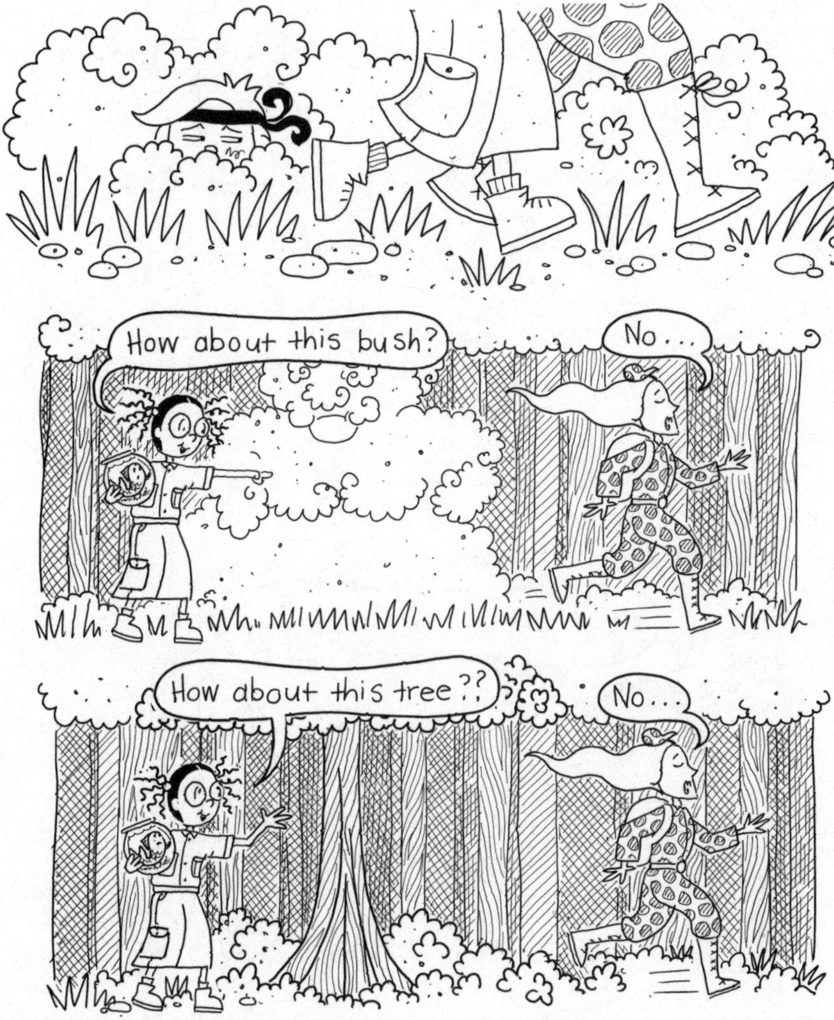
How about this bush?
No...
How about this tree??
No...

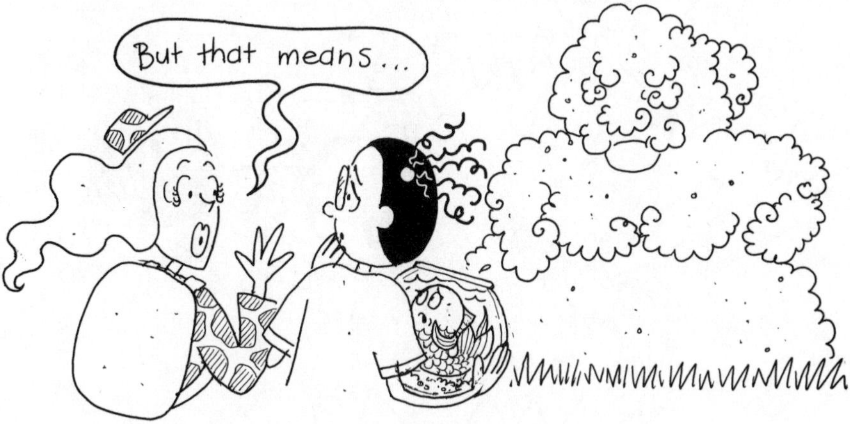
But that means...

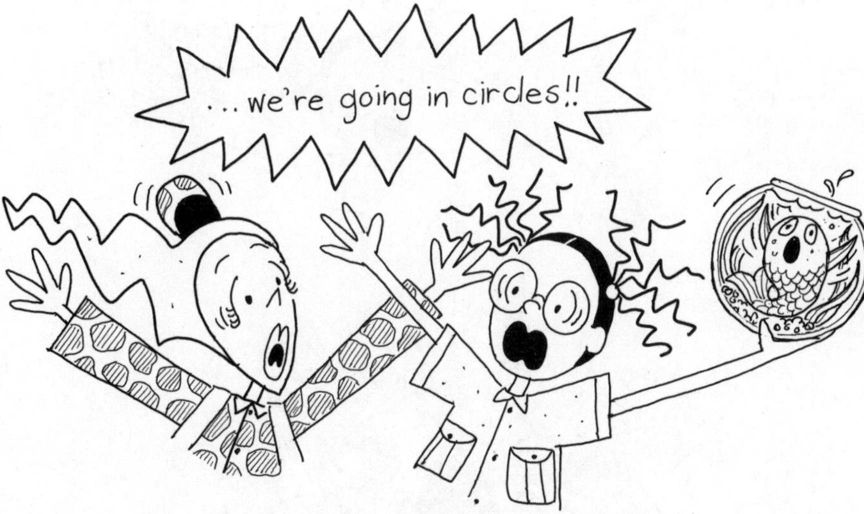
...we're going in circles!!

Meanwhile...

Meanwhile...

Should we call for help, Mr Robinson?

I have no signal...

I can track them, Mr Robinson.

You can?

Yes, I can...

Are you sure?

Yes.

All right, kids. Let's follow Bill,

and find Susie K and Clementine.

Am I supposed to be
a problem solver?

Am I supposed to be a problem
solver????

AM I SUPPOSED TO BE A
PROBLEM SOLVER??????

Yes, I am!!!!

The first thing we need to do is find the others...

73

Me too, Clementine. But it's pretty cool for now.
If you build it, she will come.

Meanwhile...

THE EUREKA MOMENT

Now we just need something to make it smokier…

Meanwhile...

The Susie K Diaries

Show Stopper!

Shamini Flint
illustrated by Sally Heinrich

SHAMINI FLINT lives in Singapore with her husband and two children. She began her career in law in Malaysia and also worked at an international law firm in Singapore. She travelled extensively around Asia for her work, before resigning to be a stay-at-home mum, writer, part-time lecturer and environmental activist, all in an effort to make up for her 'evil' past as a corporate lawyer! Shamini has written many books for adults and children, including the popular *Diary of a Soccer Star* series.

SALLY HEINRICH is an illustrator, printmaker and writer, who has published and exhibited widely in Australia and Asia. She has illustrated more than forty books, including the *Diary of a Soccer Star* series. Her picture book *One Step at a Time* was an Honour Book in the CBCA Picture Book of the Year Awards, and her most recent, *Papa Sky*, is a Notable Book. Her commissioned artwork ranges from wine labels to a mural for the Singapore Zoo and community arts projects. Sally has lived in Singapore, Sydney and Darwin and is now living in Adelaide. When she's not at her desk drawing, she is often out in the bush, walking and camping and occasionally getting lost.